D1005833

LITTLE RED Quacking Hood

Read more of Princess Pink's adventures!

Princess Pink
and the LAND OF
FAKE-BELIEVE
BRANCHES
Moldylocks and the Three Beards
SCHOLASTIC
Noah Z. Jones

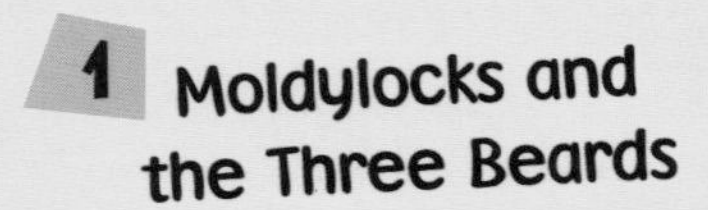
1 Moldylocks and the Three Beards

Princess Pink
and the LAND OF
FAKE-BELIEVE
BRANCHES
Little Red Quacking Hood
SCHOLASTIC
Noah Z. Jones

2 Little Red Quacking Hood

Princess Pink AND THE LAND OF FAKE-BELIEVE

LITTLE RED
Quacking Hood

by Noah Z. Jones

BRANCHES™

SCHOLASTIC INC.

To my quacky family,
Diane, Eli, and Sylvie

Library of Congress Cataloging-in-Publication Data

Jones, Noah (Noah Z.), author.
Little Red Quacking Hood / by Noah Z. Jones.
pages cm. — (Princess Pink and the Land of Fake-Believe ; 2)
Summary: In her second adventure in the Land of Fake-Believe, Princess Pink meets Scaredy-Pants Wolf, a baker whose business has been robbed by Little Red Quacking Hood—and to save the bakery Princess must figure out why the ducks are suddenly so interested in pies.
ISBN 0-545-63841-0 (pbk.) — ISBN 0-545-63842-9 (hardcover) — ISBN 0-545-63893-3 (ebook) 1. Fairy tales. 2. Bakers—Juvenile fiction. 3. Wolves—Juvenile fiction. 4. Ducks—Juvenile fiction. 5. Humorous stories. [1. Fairy tales. 2. Humorous stories. 3. Bakers and bakeries—Fiction. 4. Wolves—Fiction. 5. Ducks—Fiction.] I. Title.
PZ8.J539Li 2014
[Fic]—dc23
2013050553
ISBN 978-0-545-63842-5 (hardcover) / ISBN 978-0-545-63841-8 (paperback)

13 12 11 10 9 16 17 18 19 20/0

Printed in China 38
First Scholastic printing, September 2014

Edited by Katie Carella
Book design by Will Denton

TABLE OF CONTENTS

• CHAPTER ONE •
Can't Stand Pink

This is Princess Pink. Her first name is <u>Princess</u>. Her last name is <u>Pink</u>.

The Pink family has eight kids. Princess is the baby of the family. She has seven older brothers.

P

Princess does NOT like anything girly. And she REALLY does not like the color pink.
This blanket would be so pretty on your bed!
I can't stand pink! But I would really love a bed full of bugs!!

That night, Princess's mother tucked Princess into her new buggy bed.

But Princess did not only have a buggy blanket. She also had a bug under her blanket!

Hi, Reggie!
Hi, Princess! Your bed is much nicer than Mama Beard's bed.

Reggie the spider was not a normal bug. He came from the wacky Land of Fake-Believe. Princess met Reggie after falling through her refrigerator into that mixed-up place. Princess was afraid of the Three Beards—Mama Beard, Papa Beard, and Baby Beard. But she had made good friends there—like Reggie, Moldylocks, and Mother Moose.

Reggie jumped out of bed. He tried to drag Princess out of bed, too.

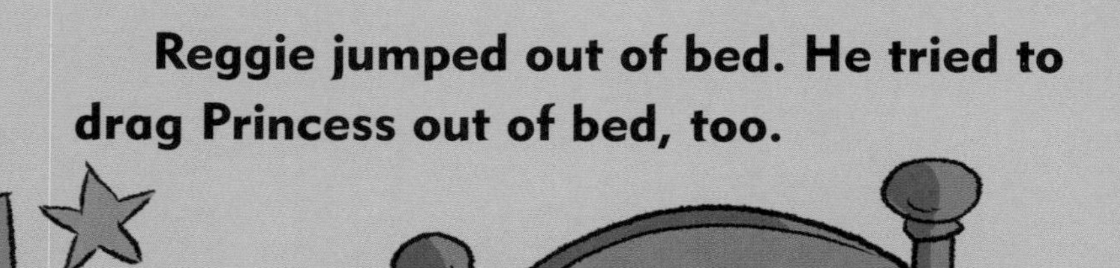

Tonight is the night, Princess! The fridge is ready to take you back to Fake-Believe!
I check every night, Reggie. Fake-Believe is never there.
It'll be there tonight. I'm sure of it. Come on!

ZZZZZ

The house was quiet. Princess and Reggie sneaked into the kitchen.

Princess put her ear to the fridge. It wasn't making its usual HUMMmmm sound. It was huffing and puffing!

HUFF
PUFF

Princess yanked open the door. It was nighttime in the Land of Fake-Believe. Princess saw a spotted fish jumping over the moon.

Hooray!
Have fun tonight! But I'm staying here—the bed will be all mine!

Princess stepped inside her fridge.

Land of Fake-Believe, here I come!

Then she climbed down the ladder.

A big shadow fell on Princess just as her feet touched the ground.
Uh-oh.

CHAPTER TWO
Scaredy-Pants Wolf

Princess turned toward the shadow. Her hand shook. She was sure it was a monster—or one of the big, bad Beards.

But it was a wolf.

AHHH!
AHHH!

Princess was surprised to see a wolf. The wolf was even more surprised to see a girl.

Princess told the scared wolf that she wasn't going to hurt him.

I'm Princess Pink. But I'm not a princess. Princess just happens to be my first name.

I'm Scaredy-Pants Wolf. Everything scares me!

Are you a baker?

Yes. And I was just on my way home. I'm very jumpy tonight because my bakery was—

Just then, Moldylocks jumped out of the bushes.

Hey, Moldylocks!
AHHH!

Princess was excited to see her friend. But before Princess could say anything, Moldylocks tackled her and Scaredy-Pants Wolf to the ground.

SHHHhhhh!
We need to hide!

Moldylocks, Scaredy-Pants Wolf, and Princess hid in the bushes.

Princess peeked through the leaves. She saw a huge, horrible shadow. The shadow was shaped like a duck.

The shadow passed by them. Princess helped her friends up.

PHEW! That was close! She almost saw us.
Who? The duck? Why were we hiding from a duck?
That wasn't just a duck. It was Little Red Quacking Hood! She's terrible!
BOO-HOO!

A crybaby wolf who is afraid of a duck? Where is the Big Bad Wolf when you need him?!

Scaredy-Pants Wolf was too upset to tell Princess the full story. But he told her enough: Little Red Quacking Hood had been stealing pies from his bakery. She even stole pies today!

Trust me, she is a bad duck!
We'll help you, Scaredy-Pants! Right, Moldylocks?
Yes! Let's head to your bakery to look for clues! Then we'll come up with a plan!

CHAPTER THREE

The BIG Bad Bakery

Big Bad Bakery
WE HAVE PIE!

The three friends ran and ran. Moldylocks led the way. She stopped in front of a very odd-looking building. It was covered in candy!

Your bakery looks good enough to eat!

It is! I eat my bakery once a week! Then I bake a new one after I eat the old one.

His tummy must be HUGE!

Princess walked inside the Big Bad Bakery. She smelled lots of yummy pies! Her stomach grumbled.

Mmm. Could I have a slice of pie?
Please help yourself. The banana cream pie is my favorite!
Scaredy-Pants Wolf makes the best pies in Fake-Believe.
PIE!
GRUMBLE

PIE!
Look! Little Red Quacking Hood took that whole stack of pies!
And she broke that pie plate.

BOO! HOO!
She always leaves such a mess!

Scaredy-Pants Wolf cleaned up the mess. Then he started baking. He talked—and cried—while he baked.

If Little Red keeps stealing pies, I might have to close my bakery.
BOO HOO!
FLOUR

Princess ate a slice of pie. Then she watched as Scaredy-Pants Wolf cried into his pie.

Gross! I bet the pie I just ate had wolf tears in it!

Princess knew she had to help her new friend. She had to save his bakery.

Let's build a trap!
That's a great idea!

We need more pies if we want to trick Little Red into coming back here right away!
Bake faster, Scaredy-Pants!
I'm baking as fast as I can!
BOO HOO!

CHAPTER FOUR

Quick-Snap Duck Trap

Scaredy-Pants Wolf baked and baked. He was so busy baking that he ALMOST stopped crying.

The three friends worked on the trap.

CLANG
ZZ-ZA-ZZ
BANG

Finally, the trap was set.

The smell of pies baking in the oven spread across the Land of Fake-Believe.

Big Bad Bakery
WE HAVE PIE!

Little Red Quacking Hood soon snuck inside the bakery.

Princess and Moldylocks were ready for her! They set off the trap.

SNAP!
UH-OH!
ALERT
ALERT

The trap worked! Little Red Quacking Hood was trapped.

CLANG

Please, please, please let me go! I must visit Grandmother Quacking Hood right away!
You're not going anywhere, Little Red!

OH, NO! LOOK!

Princess and Moldylocks turned to look where Little Red Quacking Hood pointed. That was all the time this quick-thinking duck needed. She broke free and jumped out the window.

Works every time!
CRASH

BOO HOO!
Wow! She really is tricky!

But look! That quacky duck left us a trail. Let's follow these crummy footprints!

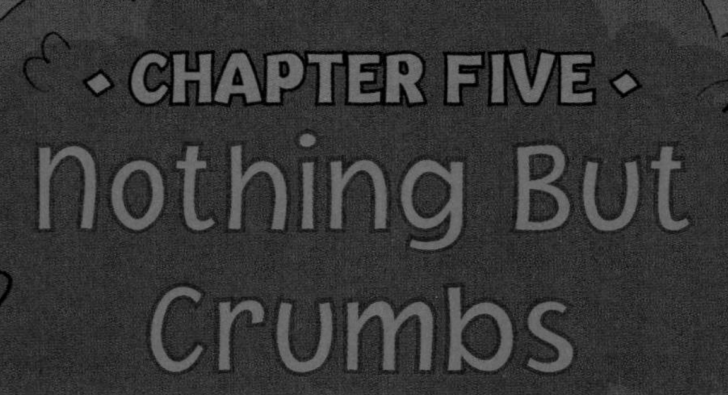

CHAPTER FIVE

Nothing But Crumbs

Oh, dear—these woods are so dark and scary. Do you really think this is a good idea?

Don't be such a scaredy-pants.

The three friends followed the long trail of footprints and crumbs into the dark and scary woods.

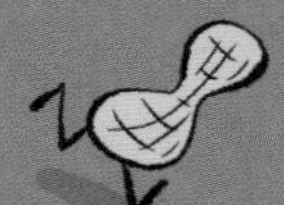

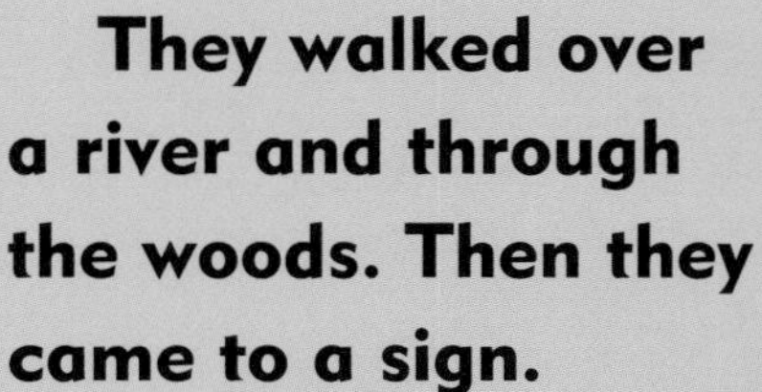

They walked over a river and through the woods. Then they came to a sign.

DUCKSVILLE
DUCKS WELCOME. ALL OTHERS TURN BACK!

Ducksville? What is this place?
Ducks live in this part of Fake-Believe. Little Red must live here, too.
We're not going in there. Are we?

Princess heard a strange noise. It was coming from behind a nearby tree.

SHUFFLE
SHUFFLE
QUACK!!

She looked behind the tree. It was Mother Moose! At least, it sort of looked like Mother Moose. He was climbing into a duck costume.

QUACK
QUACK
MM

Hi, Mother Moose! What are you doing here?
No time for questions! I must be on my way. But here—take costumes from my bag! You'll never make it into Ducksville dressed like that.
Do these costumes smell a little moldy?
MM

Princess, Moldylocks, and Scaredy-Pants Wolf looked everywhere in Ducksville. They could not find Little Red Quacking Hood.

WELCOME TO DUCKSVILLE
Can we go home now?
DUCK TRUCK

Look!
A red hood!
DUCK SCHOOL

The three friends tiptoed after Little Red Quacking Hood. She ran inside a very strange shop. It was made of brushes, combs, and scissors.

flocks of Locks
CLOSED
Come on!
Little Red's going inside!

The friends waddled across the road. They hid under an open window behind the hair salon.

This is the scariest shop on the street!! I can't look!

Princess climbed on top of Moldylocks's shoulders. She peeked inside.

• CHAPTER SIX •
Grandmother Quacking Hood

Princess saw Little Red Quacking Hood. She was handing the basket of pies to a very big duck with very big hair. It was the biggest duck Princess had ever seen.

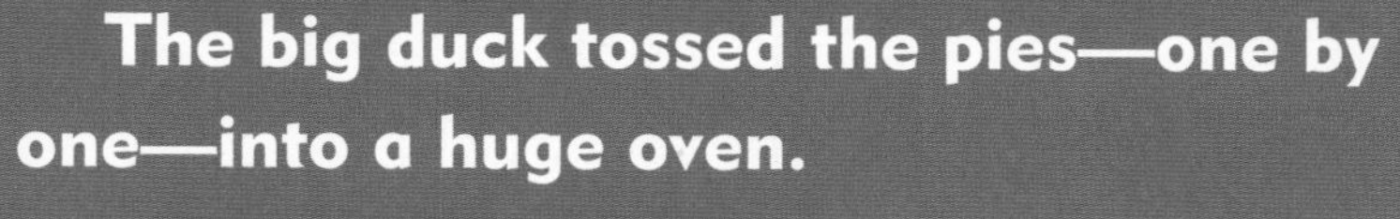

The big duck tossed the pies—one by one—into a huge oven.

Look! That's not a normal oven!
UNBAKING OVEN
Hmmm. What's an unbaking oven, Scaredy-Pants?
I don't know. I bake pies. I don't know anything about unbaking them!

Then Little Red Quacking Hood started talking to the big duck.

Grandmother Quacking Hood, the unbaking oven had better work today. Scaredy-Pants Wolf is onto us. He and his friends tried to trap me!

Do not worry, Little Red. The unbaking oven will tell us the secret ingredient soon. Then you won't have to steal any more pies.

The unbaking oven started to smoke and sputter. Grandmother Quacking Hood stomped her feet.

Not again!
UNBAKING OVEN

Little Red, go
get more pies!

Little Red Quacking Hood did as she was told. She knew not to quack back to her granny. She ran out of the salon.

Princess had heard enough. She needed to get inside the shop. She needed to find out more about the unbaking oven.

I know! I'll dress up like Little Red Quacking Hood!
Yes! Grandmother Quacking Hood will have to let her granddaughter in! All you need is a basket and a red hood.

Princess looked around. Before long she found a basket and a red hood.

She pulled the hood up over her pink hair. Then she walked right up to the front door of the Flocks of Locks salon.

CHAPTER SEVEN
All the Better to...
Don't leave me alone!
I won't. But if something goes wrong, we're going in!
flocks of Locks
CLOSED
KNOCK! KNOCK!

Grandmother Quacking Hood opened the door. She looked Princess up and down. She did not like what she saw.

Little Red, what a big bill you have!
All the better to smell the wolf's pies.
Little Red, what a big hood you have!
All the better to protect my hairdo.

Little Red, what big feet you have!
All the better to run stolen pies to you.

Princess heard shuffling noises. She also heard a quack or two. But she did not dare look around.

Soon, ducks were everywhere.
Um, Grandmother, what a lot of duck friends you have!
All the better to—

TRAP YOU WITH!!
GULP!

AHHHHH!!
QUACK!
QUACK!
QUACK!
QUACK!
QUACK!
QUACK!

◆ CHAPTER EIGHT ◆

Secret Ingredient

This wasn't part of my plan!

The ducks lifted Princess up and carried her inside the hair salon. She was trapped.

So, what do we have here? A pink spy?
I'm helping my friend. You've been stealing his pies!
We have to steal pies from the Big Bad Bakery! Ducks get bored with the same old hairdos!
HUH?

It turns out that your friend's pies are great for duck hair! The Big Bad Bakery had a pie-throwing contest. Some ducks got hit with pies. Right away, they had super fluffy and shiny feathers!

We bought the pies at first. But we ran out of money. So Little Red has been stealing them. I need the secret ingredient from those pies so I can make Flocks of Locks the best hair salon in town!

Tell me the secret ingredient! If you don't, then we'll see what happens when I feed YOU to my unbaking oven! Maybe it will unbake an answer out of you!

Princess needed more time. She needed to give Scaredy-Pants Wolf and Moldylocks time to rescue her.

WAIT! I know the secret ingredient! B-b-but . . . I have to sing it to you!

So Princess did a little dance. And she sang a little song.

A Little Red stole pies one day.
The Wolf couldn't keep her away.
The Grandmother cried, "Quack! Quack! Quack!"
As the Wolf's friends stole the pies back.
TAP!
TAPPITY!
TAP!

Grandmother Quacking Hood did not like the song. She grabbed Princess and held her over the unbaking oven.

Your time is up, pink spy!
UNBAKING OVEN
HELP!!

•CHAPTER NINE•
Tears of Joy

ROAR!

Just then Moldylocks and Scaredy-Pants Wolf rushed in. Moldylocks grabbed up Princess.

Scaredy-Pants Wolf ran over to the unbaking oven. He ate it all up with one BIG bite!

BURP!
That oven does not taste as good as my bakery!
Whoa! That was awesome!
I'm glad you're okay! Now let's get out of here!

GET THEM!
I must learn the
secret ingredient!
But I don't have a
secret ingredient!
There's nothing to tell!

Scaredy-Pants Wolf was SO scared that he curled up into a big ball. Then he started to cry.

Scaredy-Pants Wolf cried harder and harder. His tears flew all over the room. They landed on some of the ducks.

QUACKITY!
Boo Hoo!
BOO HOO!
Boo Hoo!
QUACK!
QUACKITY!

STOP!

Scaredy-Pants Wolf's tears are the secret ingredient!
BOO HOO!
It's working! Look what his tears are doing! Our salon will be the best salon in Fake-Believe!

Scaredy-Pants, could I buy your tears? I promise not to steal any more pies! AND I'll give you free haircuts anytime!
Would you mind picking up the tears from my bakery? The woods scare me.
Little Red can pick them up.

Scaredy-Pants Wolf was happy to share his tears with the ducks. He was <u>SO</u> happy that he started to cry happy tears.

As the sun was coming up, Princess said good-bye to Scaredy-Pants Wolf.

Bye, Scaredy-Pants!
Thanks for your help. I always felt bad about crying so much. But now that I know my tears can make things better, I'm going to cry even more!
BOO HOO!
Do you want a slice of pie before you go?
No thanks.
I don't think I should eat any more wolf tears!

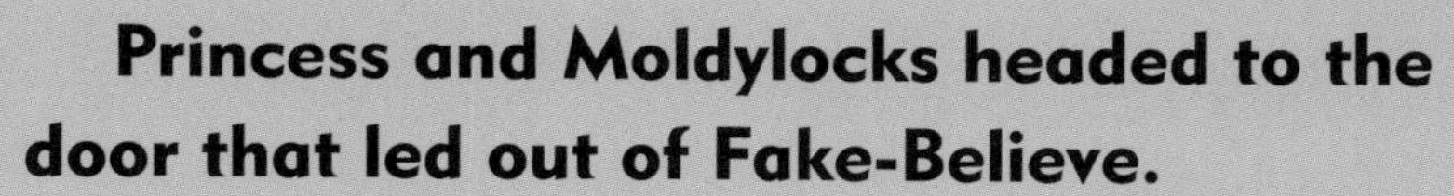

Princess and Moldylocks headed to the door that led out of Fake-Believe.

Mother Moose was there. He had a gift for Princess.

This magnet will let you return to the Land of Fake-Believe whenever you want. Just put it on your fridge. Then turn it to the left.
Cool! I'll be back before you know it!
See you soon!

Then Princess climbed up the ladder and stepped through her fridge.

Princess fell into bed. She was asleep before her head hit the pillow.

Back so soon?

Noah Z. Jones

is an author, illustrator, and animator who creates all sorts of zany characters. He hopes kids are excited to find out all about Little Red Quacking Hood! Noah has illustrated many books for children, including *Always in Trouble*, *Not Norman*, and *Those Shoes*. Princess Pink and the Land of Fake-Believe is the first children's book series that Noah has both written and illustrated.

How well do you know
THE LAND OF
FAKE-BELIEVE?

How is Scaredy-Pants Wolf similar to and different from the wolf in **Little Red Riding Hood**?

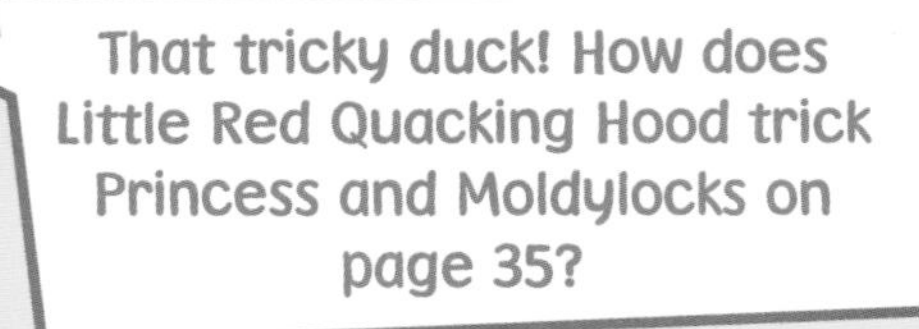
That tricky duck! How does Little Red Quacking Hood trick Princess and Moldylocks on page 35?

Reread page 27. **Knew** and **new** are homophones. These words sound the same, but are spelled differently and have different meanings. What are the meanings of **knew** and **new**?

Why do the ducks steal the pies? What is the secret ingredient in the pies?

Write a similar story from the point of view of Little Red Quacking Hood.